Catherine Rayner

ARLO

The Lion Who Couldn't Sleep

PEACHTREE

ATLANTA

Arlo was a very tired lion.

He had tried everything, but he could NOT get to sleep.

The grass was too prickly,
and the earth was too hard.
The trees were too noisy,
but the desert was too quiet.

The sun was too hot,
but the night was too cold.
His family was warm,
but they wriggled too much.

Everybody knows that
lions need a lot of sleep,
and Arlo was EXHAUSTED.

"Will I ever sleep again?" Arlo sighed.

But Arlo wasn't the only one who was awake . . .

"Of course you will," said a voice from above. "I sleep through the day when it's bright, noisy, and hot. Shall I tell you how?" And the owl began to sing . . .

Think about the places where you'd like to be,
the things that you'd do there and what you might see.

Relax your whole body, slow your breathing right down,
imagine you're sinking into the soft ground.

As you fall into calmness, so comfortable and deep,
your mind will rest and you'll drift off to sleep.

Arlo stretched, wriggled, and tried to relax,
while Owl sang her song once more.

Arlo thought of the places he would like to go and see.
He imagined bounding up mountains, wading in rivers,
and climbing enormous trees.

Then Arlo imagined he might need a rest,
so he pictured himself cuddled up with his cozy,
snoring family.

And before he knew it . . .

. . . he was sleeping too.

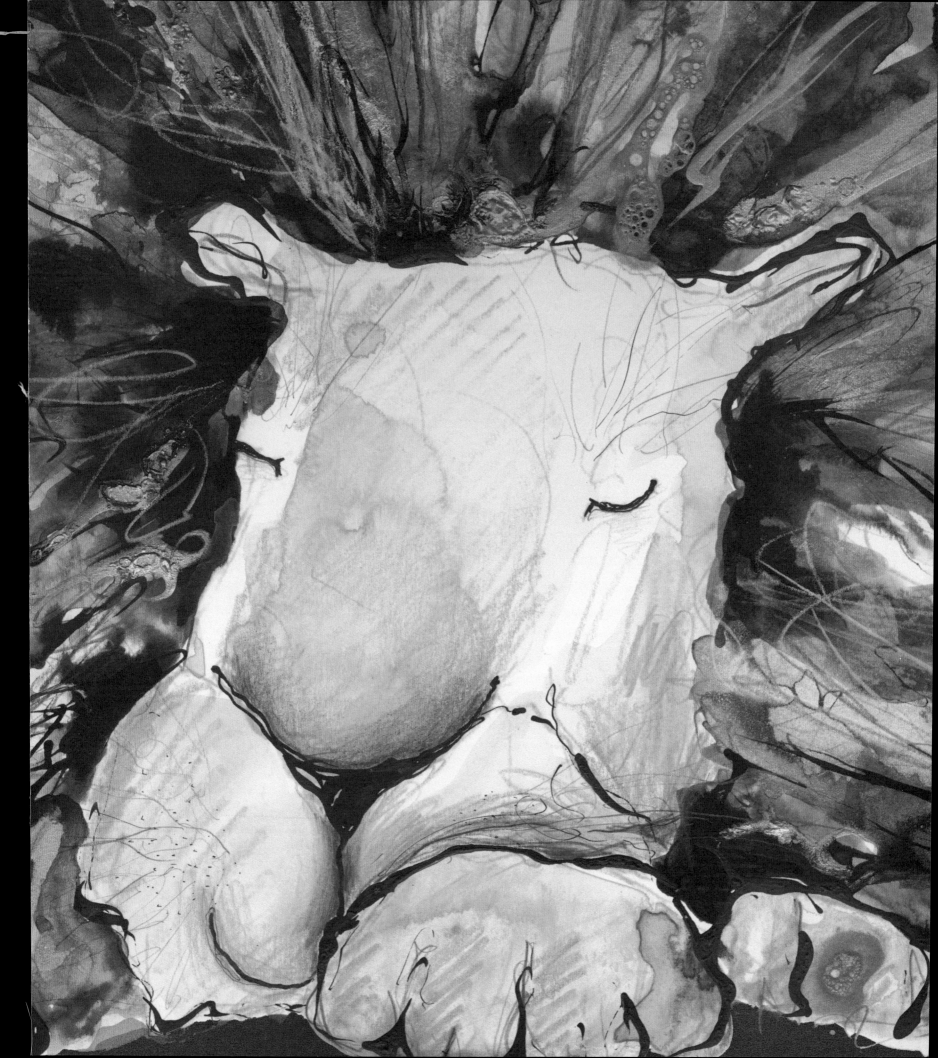

Arlo woke up feeling the sun on his coat.
He had been asleep for hours and felt
happy, fresh, and full of energy.

He couldn't wait to tell Owl.

"Little Owl?" roared Arlo. "I slept! Hooray!"

"Well done," came a tired voice from above,
"but now you've woken ME up!"

"I'm sorry," said Arlo. "Shall
I sing your song to you?"

Owl nodded her tired head,
and Arlo began to sing.

And while he sang, Owl thought of the
places she would like to go and see.
She imagined flying over waters,
soaring high and fast, and gliding
through wild forests.

Before she knew it, Owl felt starlight on her feathers.
She had slept through the day, and felt wonderful and rested.

"Hooray!" Owl and Arlo cheered.

"We're pleased YOU'VE slept, but now you've woken us all up!" the grumpy pride grumbled together.

"Sorry!" said Arlo.

"But we know what to do," hooted Owl, and Arlo and Owl sang together.

Think about the places where you'd like to be,
the things that you'd do there and what you might see.

Relax your whole body, slow your breathing right down,
imagine you're sinking into the soft ground.

As you fall into calmness, so comfortable and deep,
your mind will rest and you'll drift off to sleep.

And before long, everyone was asleep, including Arlo.

Everyone, that is, except Owl . . .

. . . who spread her wings and flew
silently into the long, quiet night.

For Emily
—C. R.

Published by
Peachtree Publishing Company Inc.
1700 Chattahoochee Avenue
Atlanta, Georgia 30318-2112
www.peachtree-online.com

First published in Great Britain in 2020 by Macmillan Children's Books, an imprint of Pan Macmillan,
a division of Macmillan Publishers International Limited
First United States version published in 2020 by Peachtree Publishing Company Inc.

Printed in China in April 2020
10 9 8 7 6 5 4 3 2 1
First Edition
ISBN: 978-1-68263-222-2

Cataloging-in-Publication Data is available from the Library of Congress

This is a story in which small explorations turn into giant adventures. It's about how the things we see aren't exactly what they seem... Sometimes they're better! (Or worse, but this is not that kind of story. Or at least not all of it is.)

This is the kind of story that starts on a perfect day for an expedition for an explorer named Sherwyn. Today he's happily wandered well away from home and stumbled over a sparkly stick. It seemed stuck.

So Sherwyn gave that stuck sparkly stick a GREAT BIG TUG...

...and POP!
It wasn't stuck.
And it wasn't a stick.
It was a tail!
A tail belonging to a GREAT BIG DRAGON...

"Aaaaghhhhh!" cried Sherwyn.

The dragon just smiled.

GREAT BIG DRAGONS are not something you see every day. Someone else might have run away, but Sherwyn was curious, a bit confused, and maybe just a teeny bit afraid. After all, this was a dragon, but a smiling dragon.

"Why are you smiling?" he said.

"Well," said the dragon, almost laughing, "I always smile when I meet someone new. It's in my nature. People I don't know are simply friends I haven't met yet. Why are you screaming?"

"Because you're a GREAT BIG DRAGON, of course! You're covered in giant, spiky scales! You're kinda scary."

"Really?" asked the smiling dragon. "Come look a little closer."

Now, when a smiling dragon asks you to come closer, it may make good sense to pause. In some stories, getting close to a dragon can be a very bad decision. This isn't that kind of story. In some stories, an explorer may be too timid to get closer to a dragon. Sherwyn isn't that kind of explorer. Sherwyn stepped closer.

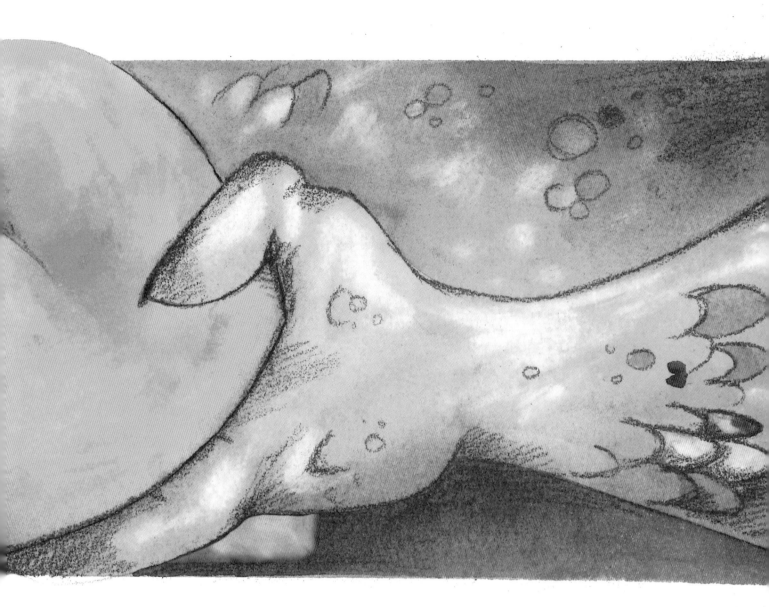

"My name is Omani and I am a Peace Dragon. I've devoted my
life to meeting and making friends and spreading a message of
peace and love. What you see as scary is actually the point of my
message," she said, slipping off a scale. "It starts with taking
time to see the whole picture. It is about greeting the world with
open eyes and an open..."

"HEART!" said a stunned Sherwyn. "You're covered in hearts!"

Sherwyn looked to see if he was covered with anything interesting. He was.

"I'm Sherwyn," he said. "I'm covered in...DIRT!"

They laughed and laughed, and the seeds of friendship were planted. From that day forward, Sherwyn and Omani set off on daily adventures, exploring every hill, field, and forest. The roots of their friendship grew deep.

One day, while resting in their favorite tree, Sherwyn finally asked Omani something that had been rolling around in his head for some time.

"You know, O, I've explored just about everywhere and I've never met a Peace Dragon. Where did you come from? Where do you live? Where've you been hiding?"

Omani laughed. "I haven't been hiding anywhere, Sherwyn. And right now I am from nowhere. I'm exploring. I've been wandering the world looking for a good place to live. You know, it is a little difficult for a dragon to find a loving home."

"WHAT?!? You have no home?" Sherwyn was stunned. "You've gotta come live in my village. You're gonna love my friends!"

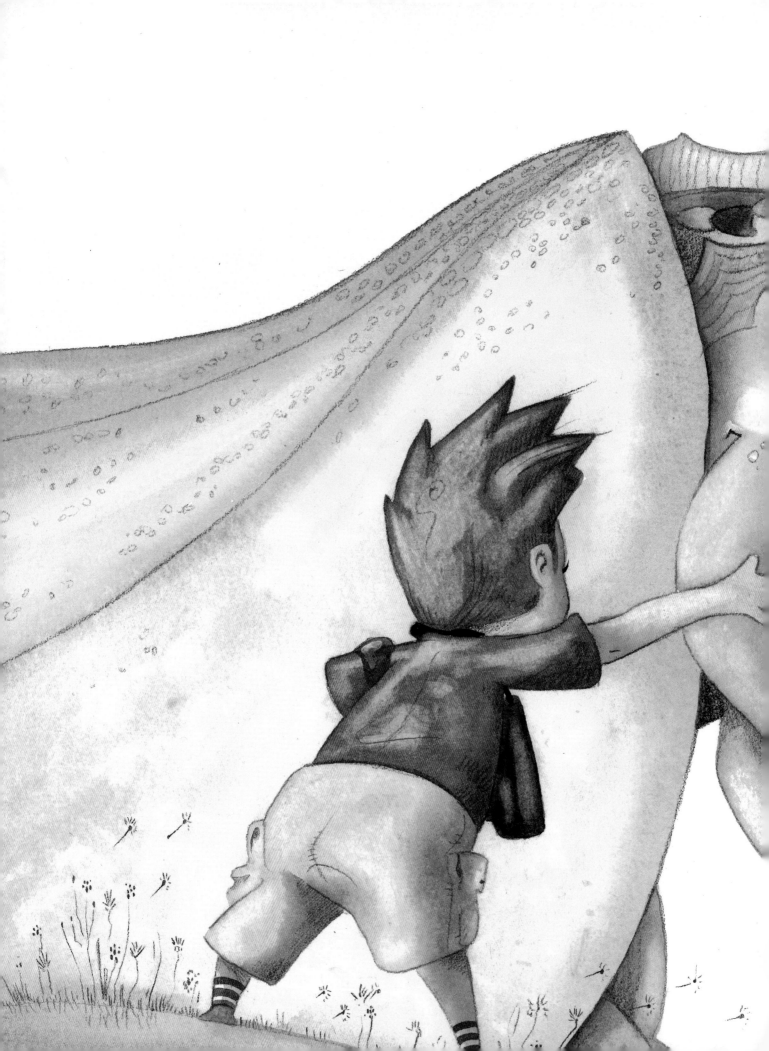

Omani smiled. "Thank you, Sherwyn. That's certainly bighearted of you, but I'm not sure this would work like you're thinking. The people in your village might not like it if you bring home a dragon. Dragons can be very scary. Remember, even you screamed when you first saw me."

Omani had a point, but Sherwyn was too excited to listen. All he could see was his friend.

"You're not scary at all! You're a Peace Dragon," Sherwyn said. "You're made of hearts and so are we. You'll see. Come on."

Sherwyn headed toward his village, assuming Omani would follow.

And follow she did. At first a bit skeptical, but then excited herself. "Maybe this time..." she hoped.

Because this is that kind of story.

Meanwhile, back in the village, everyone was going about their day as usual. A usual day consisted of people chatting in the streets, working together, lending a hand, and really just being nice to each other. They were people with kind hearts, just as Sherwyn had described them.

Sherwyn was so eager to introduce Omani to his friends that when he spotted the statue in the middle of town, he couldn't wait any longer.

"Race you to the statue!" he shouted.

Sherwyn dashed away.
Omani raced after him.

Although the villagers in Sherwyn's town were really great people, when they looked up all they saw was Sherwyn being chased by a GREAT BIG DRAGON—and the dragon was catching up! They jumped into action.

The villagers quickly formed a mad, muttering mob, mashing and smashing into each other as they prepared to battle.

"Aaaaghhhhh!"

"It's a beast!"

"Sherwyn, we'll save you!"

"STOP!"
cried Sherwyn.
"Please, stop."

Bumping and banging into itself,
the crowd stopped only inches
away from bashing into the two
frightened friends.

"This is my friend Omani," Sherwyn
explained. "She's a Peace Dragon."

"Dragons aren't peaceful!"
"Dragons are scary!"
"Dragons are nasty!"

Nobody was listening at all. Until...

"Wait! Look," said one gentle voice in the crowd, pointing at their shadow.
"Are we a nasty dragon?"

The whole crowd fell silent as they looked.
They were the only nasty dragon in sight.

1

Slowly the villagers began shuffling apart, and the shadowy shapes became friendly, familiar faces.

Sherwyn showed them Omani's scales.
"She's made of all hearts."

Sherwyn told them why they were running.
"We were racing to meet you."

And very quickly that GREAT BIG DRAGON disappeared and Omani the Peace Dragon appeared. The villagers' eyes were opened and they could see what Sherwyn saw. They felt their hearts turn toward love. Omani felt their love too.

She had finally found a loving home.

Sherwyn and Omani kept exploring, and wherever they went they shared Omani's message. The village embraced her message too. You might say Omani became the heart of the village.

In fact, Omani's message is also the heart of this story, and hopefully one day, it will be the heart of this world. Because while things can sometimes seem strange and scary, an open heart may reveal that they are friendly and loving. And if we choose, we can all live that kind of story.

"Greet the world with
open eyes and an open heart.
Use your heart as your compass
and keep your compass
pointed toward love."
—Omani